Gavin and Errol and Sophie

and Sushma and David and Kate

and Robert and Alison are . . .

...Starting
School

Janet and Allan Ahlberg

VIKING KESTREL

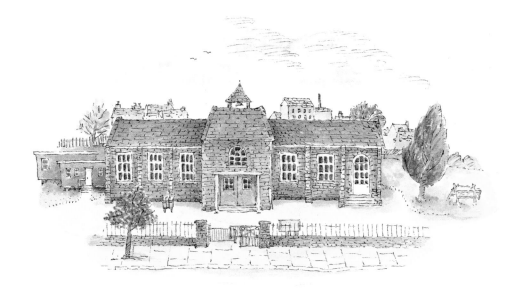

For
Val Dwelly, who gave us the idea
and
Birstall Riverside Primary School, who let us in.

VIKING KESTREL
Published by the Penguin Group
27 Wrights Lane, London W8 5TZ, England
Viking Penguin Inc., 40 West 23rd Street, New York, New York 10010, USA
Penguin Books Australia Ltd, Ringwood, Victoria, Australia
Penguin Books Canada Ltd, 2801 John Street, Markham, Ontario, Canada L3R 1B4
Penguin Books (NZ) Ltd, 182-190 Wairau Road, Auckland 10, New Zealand
Penguin Books Ltd, Registered Offices: Harmondsworth, Middlesex, England

First published 1988

Copyright © Janet and Allan Ahlberg, 1988

Library of Congress Catalog Card Number: 88–50053

Consultant Designer: Douglas Martin
Printed and bound in Great Britain by
William Clowes Limited, Beccles and London

The First Day

The children wait
in the playground

with their moms and
dads and brothers and

sisters ... and a puppy.

The bell rings.

Gavin and Errol
and Sophie and

Sushma  and David

and Kate and Robert and Alison

go into the school

and meet their teacher.

They hang
their hats and
coats in the cloakroom, take a look

 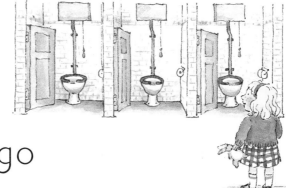

at the toilets and go
into the classroom. They sit on the mat
with the rest of the class.

The teacher takes attendance and collects the lunch money.

She shows the children around the

classroom,  and the parents too.

 In the classroom there are

tables chairs and

drawers for the children to keep their

things in. There is...

a book
corner

a home
corner

an interest
table

a box of
dressing up clothes

and a baby rabbit

in a rabbit hutch.

During the morning  Gavin

and Errol  and Sophie

and Sushma and David

and Kate

and Robert and

Alison get used to the classroom

 and the rabbit gets used

to them.

At play time . . .

they go out to play.

At lunch time they eat their lunches.

In the afternoon they draw pictures,

go out to play again and have

singing in the gym.

At the end of the day they
clean up,
listen to a story on the mat,

put on their hats and coats –
and go home.

The Second Day

The next day Gavin and Errol and

Sophie and Sushma and David and

Kate and Robert and Alison

go to school again.

  In the morning they draw a picture and do some writing in their new books.

 After that they have music and exercise in the gym.

Errol's mom plays the piano.

At play time Robert loses his hat ... and Alison finds it.

Errol bangs his knee,  and the teacher rubs it better.

Gavin and Sushma and David go climbing.

Kate <u>thinks</u> about climbing.

In the afternoon the children make
some models.

They show them to the
head teacher, listen to a story
on the mat and go home.

The First Week

As the days go by,

the children

get more used to the school.

On Wednesday they go into the gym
for assembly.

They listen to the
singing and say
a prayer.

They watch some older children put on
a play.

On Thursday they start learning to read.

Run, run as fast as you can.

"Stop, stop little boy" Said the horse

He jumped onto the fox's back.

Gavin can read already.
He brings his book from  home to show the teacher.

Errol brings his <u>tooth</u> to show the teacher.
It came out in the night.

On Friday they go swimming in the school pool.

The water is warm and not deep. Robert  and Sushma and Kate jump up and down.

David and Sophie walk in down the steps.  Errol <u>thinks</u> about walking in.

In the afternoon Kate and Sushma and
David do cooking
with David's mom.

They make 12 little cakes,

3 big cakes

...and a mess.

Time Goes By

The next week Gavin  and

Errol and Sophie

and Sushma

 and David  and Kate

 and

Robert and Alison . . .

choose a name for the rabbit.

Benjamin
Bertie   Peter
Ronald   Snuffles
Whiskers Flop
Bun   Timmy
Mr Grimshaw

They draw rabbit   pictures,

Kate

Robert

make rabbit models,

bake rabbit biscuits,

listen to rabbit stories on the mat, and do

lots more rabbit

things besides.

My name is Ronald

Run, rabbit
Run, rabbit
Run, run, run!

shop

The week after that the children have their photographs taken.

And the week after that   Gavin loses a glove,

and Alison learns to swim;

Sophie reads  a book,

and Sushma shows her sari

and her Diva  lamp.

Robert <u>thinks</u> about being in a

hallowe'en play.

And sometimes the children

are happy,

and sometimes they are sad;

sometimes puzzled – or sleepy –

or grumpy – or lumpy – or spotty!

Sometimes

the teacher is not

cheerful either.

Christmas Comes

In the last week of school all the classes
put on a play
about baby Jesus.

Everybody  has a part,

and all the moms
and dads come
to watch.

On the last <u>day</u> of school
the children bring cakes

and chips,

hot dogs,  sandwiches

and treats, and have a party

in the classroom.

Then Gavin and Errol

and Sophie

and Sushma

and Kate

and David

and Robert and Alison

go home ...

and the holiday begins.